D0568234

Boswell, Addie K.,
Five on the bed /
[2020]
33305251448076
ca 03/12/21

Five on the Bed

BY ADDIE BOSWELL

WEST
MARGIN
PRESS

There is
ONE
on the
bed.

of the Honorable J
BRAY
NORT
and filed with the A
to quiet title in the
the complaint on fi

ONE on the bed and

ONE below the bed.

Now
there
are
TWO.

We sustained
ter we got o
ONED to answer the Complai
not served with this Summo
r the service of this Summons
Judgment will be taken against y
irst cactus injury righ
the car. My 10-year-
ing around the garde
0001327
section 507, because the judgment
of, real property situated within such
unty of Monroe
explodes into the colorful
e park is famous, but also
side. In a tent. The first
d pitched a tent was the
my living room, holding a
my husband did most of
attorney
failure to
Compla
Date
SANTIA
Tel.: (585)

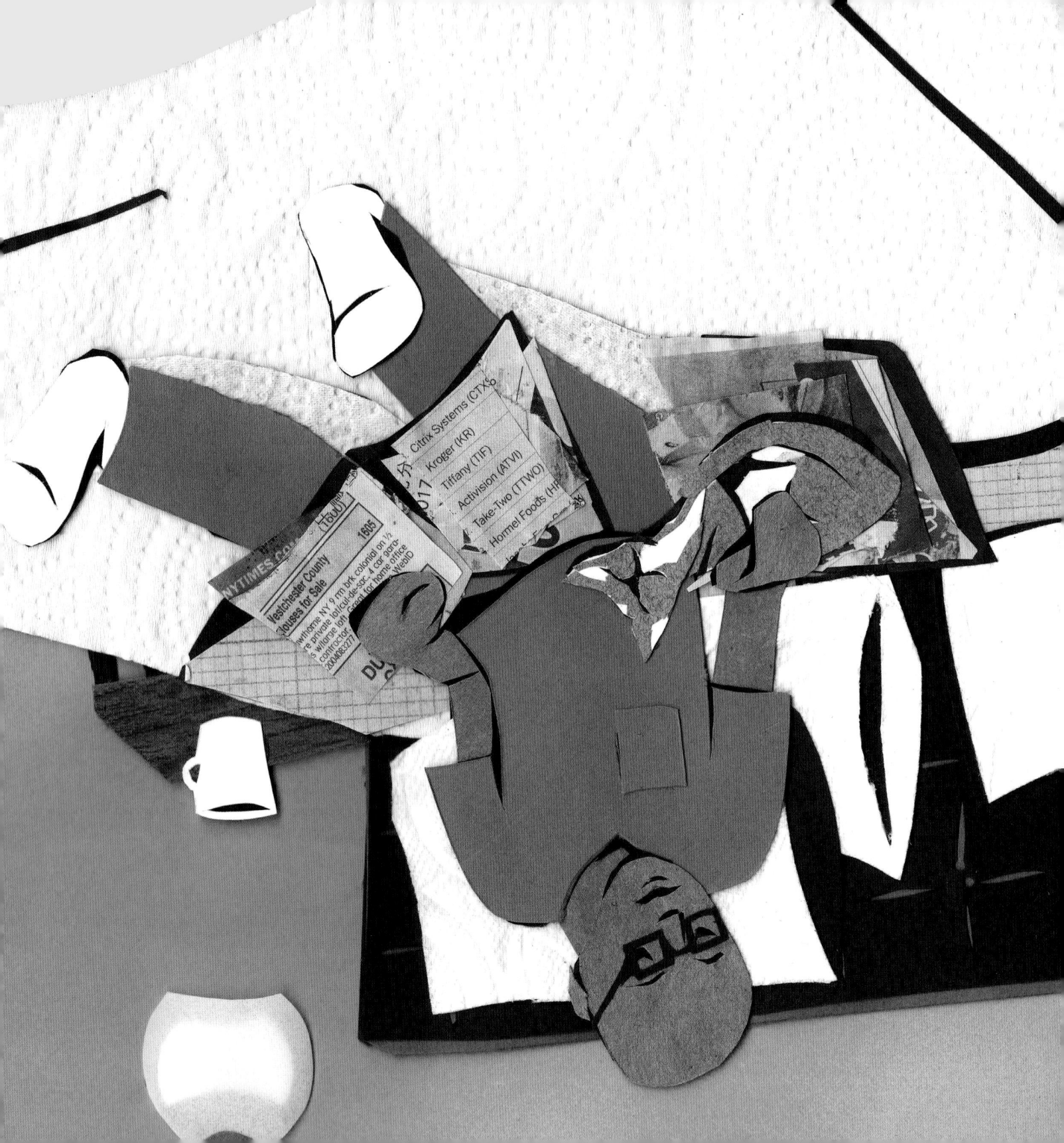
Citrix Systems (CTXS)
Kroger (KR)
Tiffany (TIF)
Activision (ATVI)
Take-Two (TTWO)
Hormel Foods (HR
Westchester County
Houses for Sale
1995

TWO
on the bed
and
TWO
below.

HOW MUCH $585,000
SIZE 3,135 square feet
PRICE PER SQUARE FOOT
wiping down seat ar
be any

FOUR
on the bed!

shower. One of the ro
nected to a paneled
with octagonal windo
skylight. The breezew
third bedroom above
with an en suite bath
has a shower. There
lkout basement.
OR SPACE A de
371
and
our scheme didn't
ave to decide on the
ake the flight and be

Uh-oh...
ONE...

TWO...
San Juan
Angahuan
PARÍCUTIN
detached three-car garage.
PER SQUARE FOOT

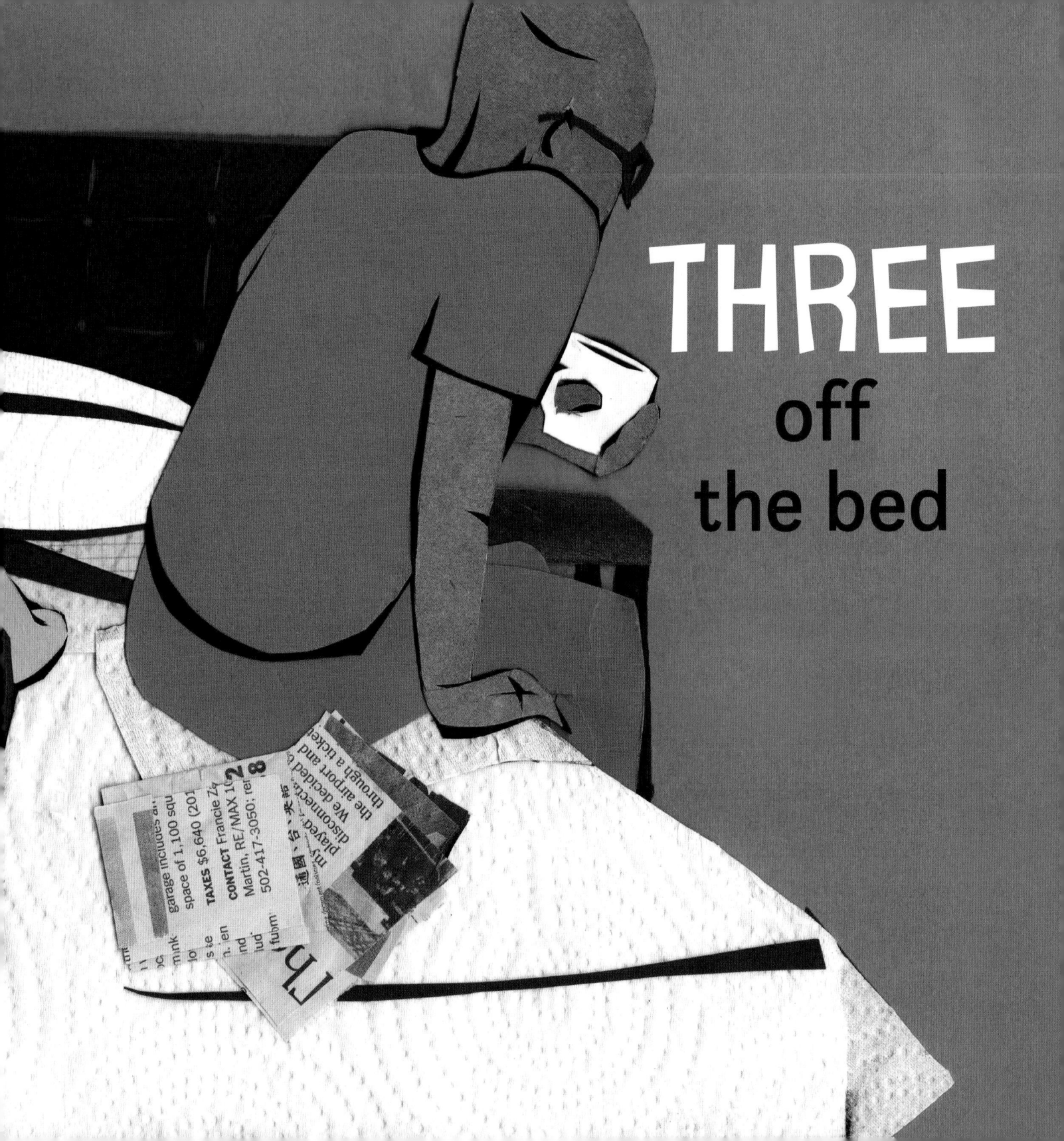

THREE
off the bed

and
ONE
above!

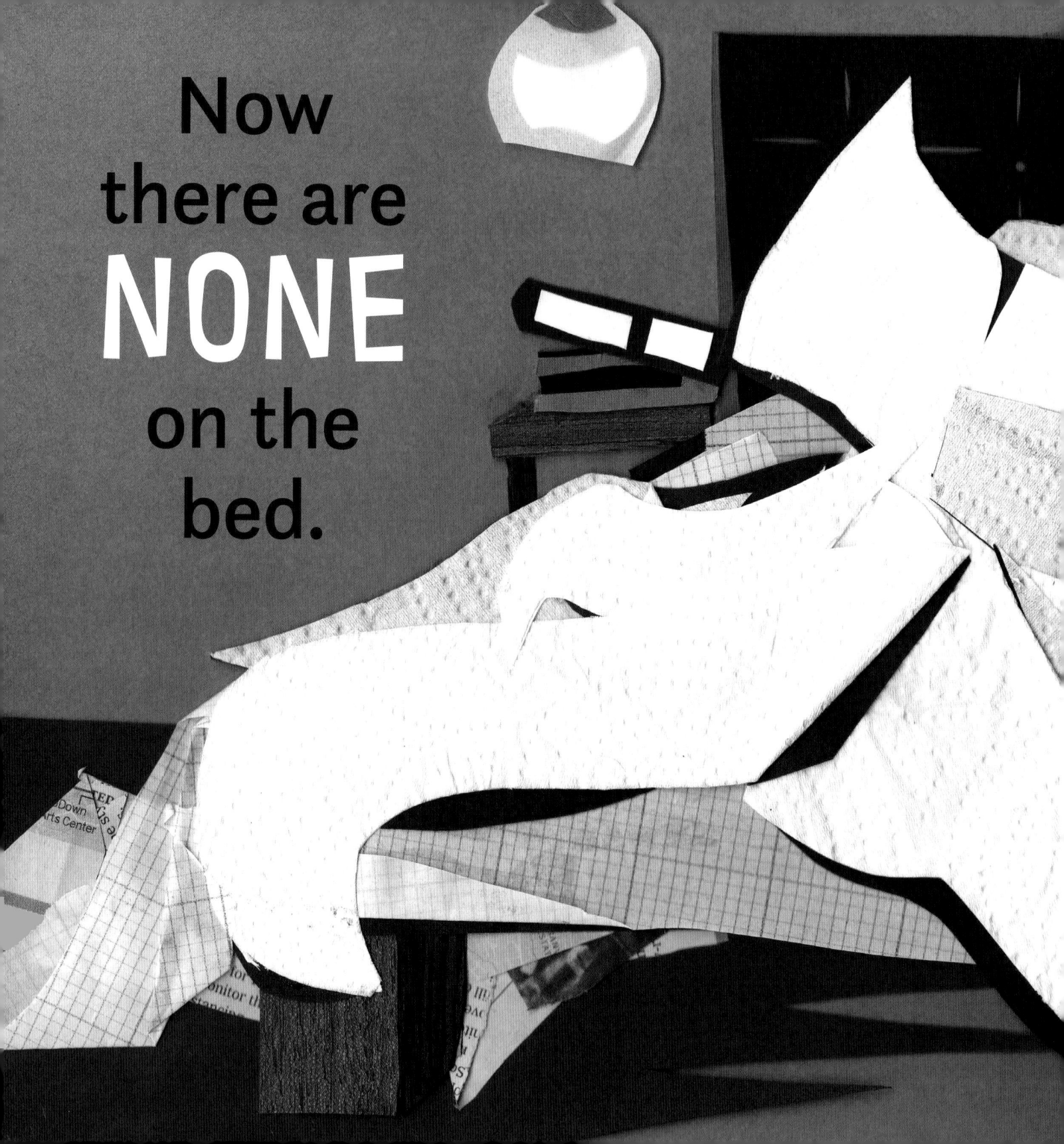
Now
there are
NONE
on the
bed.

top | $500 at Uhuru
uhurudesign.com
■ Is the weight important? Yes, a
should be robust enough that it do
Mr. Dorsey said, but light enough t
move between rooms.

tive of the Gavi Allia
started by Bill a
works to get vac
noted that one
was discovere
lab, transferr
and then pr
"That's

NONE?

ONE!

And TWO...

and

THREE...

and FOUR...

FIVE ON THE—

Shhhh...

FIVE on the bed, fast asleep.

Dedicated to my four: Adam, Immie, Beazle, and Cucamonga.

Text & Illustrations © 2020 by Addie Boswell

Edited by Michelle McCann

All rights reserved. No part of this book may be reproduced or transmitted in any form or by any means, electronic or mechanical, including photocopying, recording, or by any information storage and retrieval system, without written permission of the publisher.

Library of Congress Cataloging-in-Publication Data

Names: Boswell, Addie K., author, illustrator.
Title: Five on the bed / Addie Boswell.
Description: [Berkeley] : West Margin Press, [2020] | Audience: Ages 3. | Audience: Grades K–1. | Summary: A young girl, her parents, and their dog and cat appear on, under, and next to the bed as they all get ready to sleep in this counting book featuring cut paper illustrations.
Identifiers: LCCN 2020018749 (print) | LCCN 2020018750 (ebook) | ISBN 9781513264288 (hardback) | ISBN 9781513264295 (ebook)
Subjects: CYAC: Family life—Fiction. | Bedtime—Fiction. | Beds—Fiction. | Cats—Fiction. | Dogs—Fiction. | Counting.
Classification: LCC PZ7.B65125 Fiv 2020 (print) | LCC PZ7.B65125 (ebook) | DDC [E]—dc23
LC record available at https://lccn.loc.gov/2020018749
LC ebook record available at https://lccn.loc.gov/2020018750

Proudly distributed by Ingram Publisher Services

Printed in China
24 23 22 21 20 1 2 3 4 5

Published by West Margin Press

WEST MARGIN PRESS

WestMarginPress.com

WEST MARGIN PRESS
Publishing Director: Jennifer Newens
Marketing Manager: Angela Zbornik
Project Specialist: Gabrielle Maudiere
Editor: Olivia Ngai
Design & Production: Rachel Lopez Metzger